PEACH
BLOSSOM
SPRING

PEACH BLOSSOM SPRING

ADAPTED FROM A CHINESE TALE

BY FERGUS M. BORDEWICH
ILLUSTRATED BY YANG MING-YI

GREEN TIGER PRESS
Published by Simon & Schuster
New York   London   Toronto   Sydney   Tokyo   Singapore

GREEN TIGER PRESS
Simon & Schuster Building, Rockefeller Center
1230 Avenue of the Americas, New York, New York 10020
Text copyright © 1994 by Fergus M. Bordewich
Illustrations copyright © 1994 by Yang Ming-Yi
GREEN TIGER PRESS is an imprint of Simon & Schuster.
Manufactured in the United States of America

10   9   8   7   6   5   4   3   2   1

Library of Congress Cataloging-in-Publication Data
Bordewich, Fergus M. Peach blossom spring / by Fergus M. Bordewich ;
illustrated by Yang Ming-Yi.   p.   cm.   Summary: When he
accidentally discovers a beautiful hidden valley inhabited
by contented people, a fisherman is asked to return but
only if he tells no one where he's been.
[1. Fishers—Fiction. 2. China—Fiction.]   I. Yang, Ming-Yi, ill.   II. Title.
PZ7.B64833Pe   1994
[E]—dc20   92-19676   CIP   ISBN: 0-671-78710-1

For Chloe La Verne, my beloved daughter.
May she always find blossoms in her path.

—F.M.B.

To Richard Inglis and his wife

—Y.M.Y.

One day a fisherman from the city of Wu-ling was rowing along an unfamiliar stream. He was paying no attention to how far he was going, when suddenly he came to a grove of blossoming peach trees stretching along both banks.

Their falling blossoms swirled and danced in the summer breeze, and their fragrance was so delicious that he stopped to enjoy it. After awhile he discovered a spring at the end of the grove. Nearby a cave led into the mountainside. A faint light seemed to come from within, and he decided to see where it led.

At first the cave was so narrow that the fisherman could hardly get through, but after he had continued for some distance the passageway opened up into daylight.

As the fisherman emerged, a hidden valley appeared before him, as if in a dream. Tidy cottages stood amid rich fields and beautiful ponds. Farmers were stacking hay on curving terraces, bending and folding, bending and folding, chattering cheerfully to each other as they worked.

Even the trees seemed friendly. There were pomegranates and palms, plum trees and willows. There were forests of slender bamboo, and strange feathery trees that the fisherman had never seen before in the outside world.

Wrens and swallows chirped and twittered among the branches, while flocks of colorful birds wheeled and whirled high overhead. Some of them had tiny flutes tied to their wings, so that as they swooped and dove, the air hummed and whistled with a delicate music more beautiful than anything the fisherman had ever heard.

When the farmers saw the fisherman, they gathered around excitedly and asked where he had come from. When he told them, they were astonished. They knew nothing of the outside world, and none of them had ever seen a stranger before.

They explained that the valley's fields always produced just enough to eat, that the weather in the valley was always just right, and that everyone there treated his neighbors with just the proper amount of kindness and respect.

"We call our valley Peach Blossom Spring," said one.

All the villagers in turn invited the fisherman to their homes for food and drink. They explained that their grandparents' grandparents' grandparents had come to the valley to escape the cruelty of an ancient emperor. After reaching the valley, they had never left it again.

The fisherman related all that had happened in the hundreds of years since their ancestors had come to Peach Blossom Spring. The villagers were astonished at what he told them.

"People wear silk robes embroidered with dragons now, and they eat silkworm pie for dinner," the fisherman boasted, although he was rather poor and could not afford such luxuries himself. "They have more than one hundred different kinds of tea to drink, and they print whole stories on paper with blocks of wood, and when they make war, they have a powder that can blow up a whole town!"

The villagers sighed and murmured at everything they heard.

"Why should we ever leave here," they said to each other. "What the stranger tells us sounds wonderful indeed, but we could never be as happy anywhere else."

It surprised the fisherman that although there were huge carp swimming in the ponds, none of his hosts ate fish.

"No one here knows how to catch them," the villagers said sadly.

"Let me show you," the fisherman offered.

The next day he dropped a line into a pond and soon pulled up a wriggling carp. The villagers said they had never tasted anything so good in their lives!

"Please stay here with us," the villagers pleaded.

The fisherman thought of his poor home in the city, with its crowds and its noise. Then he looked around him at the happy villagers and the sunny fields, and at the wonderful birds making their strange music overhead.

"I'll just go home and get my things," the fisherman said eagerly.

"It is very difficult to find this valley," the villagers warned him. "You must promise not to tell anyone that we are here, or you will never be able to find your way back at all."

The fisherman gave them his word that he wouldn't tell a soul.

He made his way back through the cave. He found his boat where he had left it, and then retraced his route downstream, carefully leaving markers along the way so that he would be able to find his way to Peach Blossom Spring again.

When he reached the city, the fisherman hurried to his home and gathered up his belongings.

On the way out of town the fisherman ran into his old friend Little Wang, who mended nets for a living.

"Where have you been?" Little Wang asked. "I was worried about you!"

The fisherman bit his lip. He was so excited that he could hardly hold his tongue. He remembered his promise to the people of the valley, but it couldn't hurt to tell just one person, he thought.

He told Little Wang about the cave and the secret valley, and the kindly villagers and the huge carp.

"It's the most wonderful place I've ever heard of!" Wang exclaimed. "Please let me go back with you!"

It would be nice to have the company of an old friend at Peach Blossom Spring, the fisherman thought. So he agreed.

"But you mustn't tell another soul!" he said.

"Of course not!" Little Wang replied.

A little farther along the way, they ran into Lanky Li, the proprietor of their favorite teahouse.

"Where are you going?" Lanky Li asked, curiously eyeing the two men who were loaded down with all the fisherman's nets and fishing lines and floats.

The fisherman sighed. As long as he had already told Little Wang, he decided it wouldn't make much difference if he told someone else.

Lanky Li's jaw fell open when he heard about Peach Blossom Spring.

"Won't you please allow me to come with you?" Lanky Li begged.

"How can we say no?" Little Wang whispered to the fisherman.

"All right," the fisherman sighed. "But let's hurry before we meet anyone else."

A little farther down the road, as luck would have it, they encountered Fat Chang, who made the tastiest spicy bean curd in the city. Before anyone could stop him, Lanky Li had blurted out the story of Peach Blossom Spring.

"Think how nice it would be to have Fat Chang's bean curd when we get to Peach Blossom Spring," Little Wang said.

That made sense to the fisherman, so he told Fat Chang to gather up his pots and pans and join them too.

By the time the fisherman, Little Wang, Lanky Li and Fat Chang reached the river, hundreds of people were tagging along behind them. Some were carrying their belongings in great heaps on their backs. Others were tugging heavily laden donkeys. Still others were pushing wheelbarrows piled high with furniture. There were rich people and poor people, and old people and young people, and whole families with their babies. All of them were shoving and yelling at each other to get out of the way.

What would the villagers say? the fisherman wondered and worried. How would all these people even fit into Peach Blossom Spring?

It took dozens of boats to carry everyone. More and more joined them, until by the time they arrived at the forest of peach trees, there was a traffic jam of boats that extended for miles along the stream.

"Hurry up! Hurry up!" people kept shouting at the fisherman. "We're hungry and tired. Won't we ever get to Peach Blossom Spring?"

The fisherman was suddenly confused. Nothing looked quite the way he had remembered it. He searched for the markers he had left, but everything was covered with peach blossoms as far as the eye could see.

The city people were very impatient. They jumped out of their boats and ran off in every direction, scattering peach blossoms and branches and stones until any hope of finding the markers was gone. The fisherman now knew that they would never find Peach Blossom Spring.

Sighing, he sat down in his little boat, dropped a line in the water, and sat watching the peach blossoms as they drifted in the summer breeze like snow. It was the most beautiful sight he had ever seen.

Many people who have heard the fisherman's tale have set off in search of Peach Blossom Spring. But no one has ever found it.